HODDER CHILDREN'S BOOKS

First published in Great Britain
in 2019 by Hodder & Stoughton
First published in paperback in 2020

Copyright © Chloë and Mick Inkpen, 2019

Hodder Children's Books
An imprint of Hachette Children's Group
Part of Hodder & Stoughton
Carmelite House
50 Victoria Embankment
London, EC4Y 0DZ

A CIP catalogue record for this book is
available from the British Library.

ISBN 978 1 444 95034 2

1 3 5 7 9 10 8 6 4 2

Printed in China

An Hachette UK Company
www.hachette.co.uk
www.hachettechildrens.co.uk

Mrs Blackhat
and the ZoomBroom!

Chloë and Mick Inkpen

Hodder
Children's
Books

Mrs Blackhat flicks the switch
on her new ZoomBroom
and taps the app on her
WiTCHwatch.
'Welcome to ZoomBroom,'
says the ZoomBroom
and it sings a silly song.

'Climb on, everyone!'
says Mrs Blackhat.

Dreams all come true on the ZoomBroom! Oooh what a view from the ZoomBroom! There's so

to do, for me and for you! So won't you come too on the ZoooooooooooooooooooooomBroom!

'Who needs magic when you've got **technology!**' laughs Mrs Blackhat.

But she tucks her magic wand up her sleeve just in case and taps the GO button.

Oops! She has forgotten to unplug.

The ZoomBroom hovers
 above the garden.
It seems to be waiting.
 'I wonder what this button does,'
says Mrs Blackhat.

She taps a pink button
on her WiTCHwatch.
'You have selected
Bubblematic!
Enjoy!' says the
ZoomBroom.

They rise into the clouds
and bubbles fill the air.

'Lovely!' says Mrs Blackhat.

The ZoomBroom sings its
silly song again.

Oooh what a view from the ZoomBroom! There's so much to do, for me and for you! So won't you co

The purple button
is even better.
'You have selected
Acrobatic!
Hang on tight!'
'Wheeeeeeee!'
shrieks Mrs Blackhat,
'isn't this fun!'

There's so much to do, for me and for you! So won't you c

ooooooommBroom!

who

But the red button is best of all!
'Experienced pilots only!'
says the ZoomBroom.
She presses it anyway.

Into the sky they zoom at **supersonic speed** . . .

. . . and all around the world in just one afternoon!

But passing New York
the ZoomBroom begins to splutter
and stops singing its silly song.
Then all its lights go out.
The batteries are running out.

'Uh oh!' says Mrs Blackhat.

Mrs Blackhat is pressing buttons. But nothing is happening!

She remembers her magic wand!

'Eye of newt
and ping pong bat.
Please don't let us
all go splat!'

(It is the best
she can do in the
time available.)

The ZoomBroom
plugs itself into
**The
Statue
Of
Liberty!**

Just in time
the lights blink into life
and the ZoomBroom
comes to a halt,
hovering above the water
while its batteries
recharge.

Mrs Blackhat hits the home button on her WiTCHwatch.

Time to go.

High above the clouds they climb.

...oomBroom! There's so much to do, for me and for you! So won't you come too on the Zooooooooooo...

'You have reached your destination,' says the ZoomBroom.

Home at last.

But look!
There is one more button
blinking on the WiTCHwatch.
'Aha!' says Mrs Blackhat.

Gulp!

'I love technology!'
squeals Mrs Blackhat.

So they boogywoogy
all night long
and they all join in
the silly song
while Mrs Blackhat
waves her wand . . .

what a view from the Zoo

...and fills the sky with

magic!